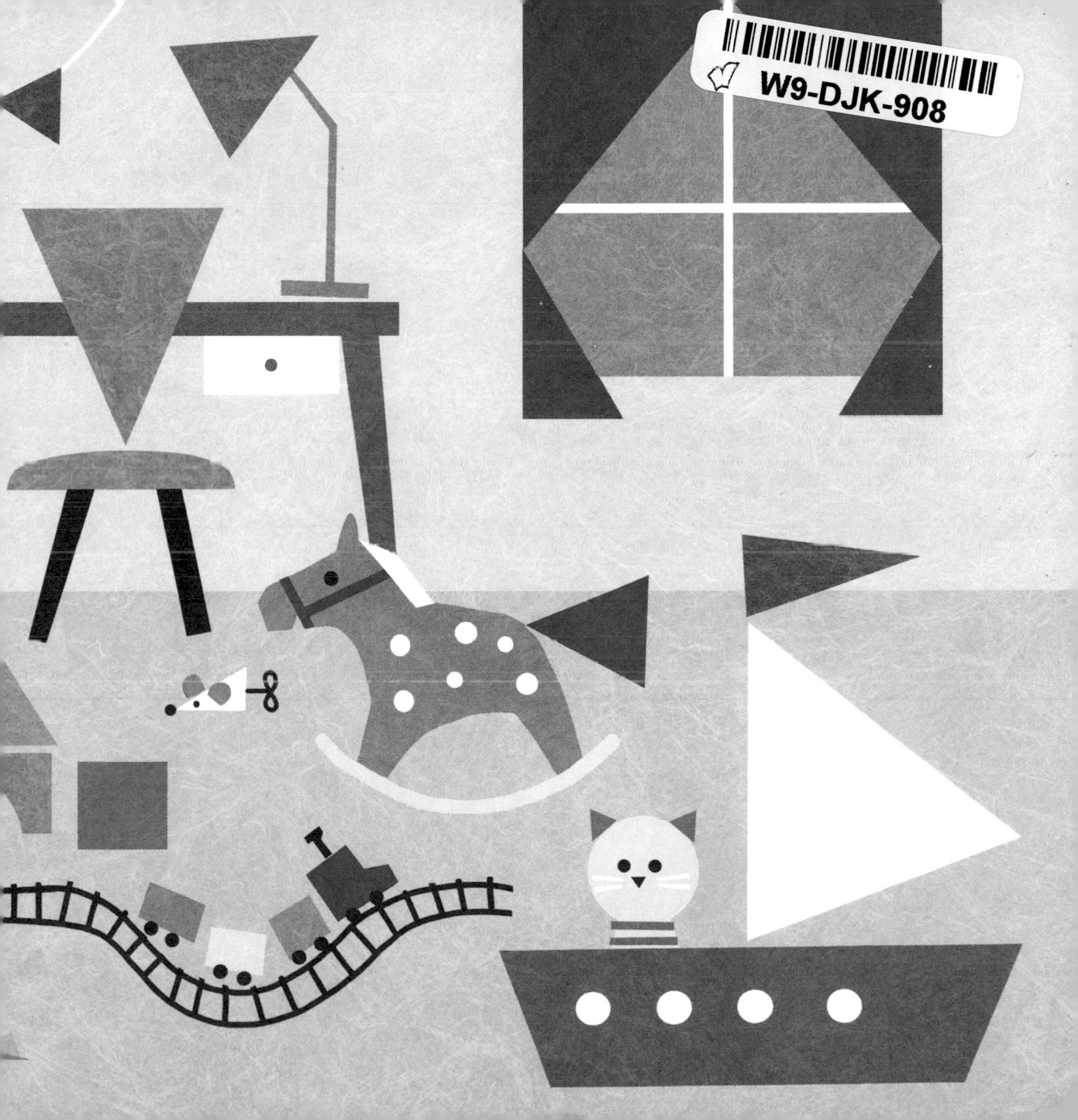

Squares, squares!
Do you see
the squares?

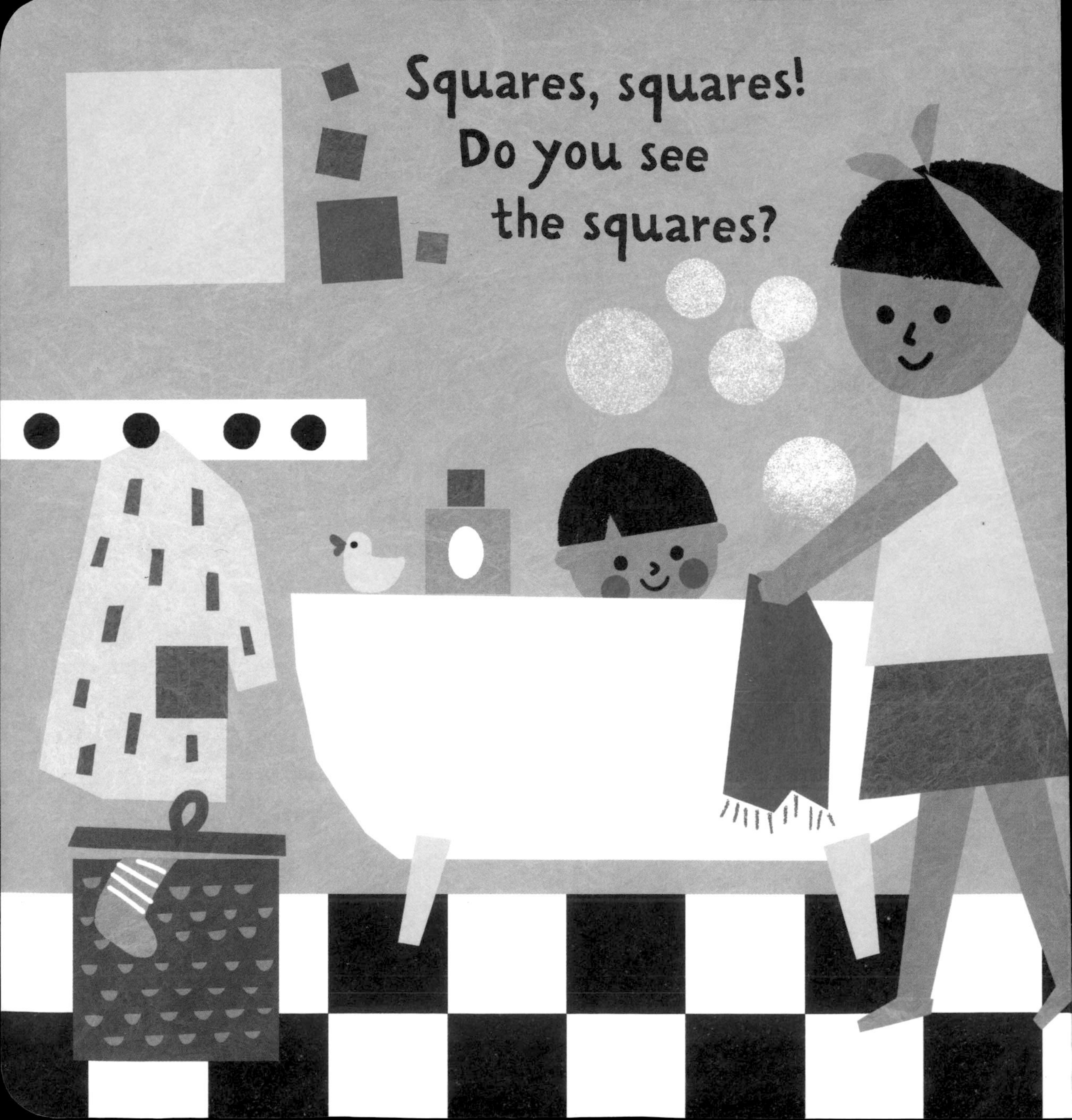

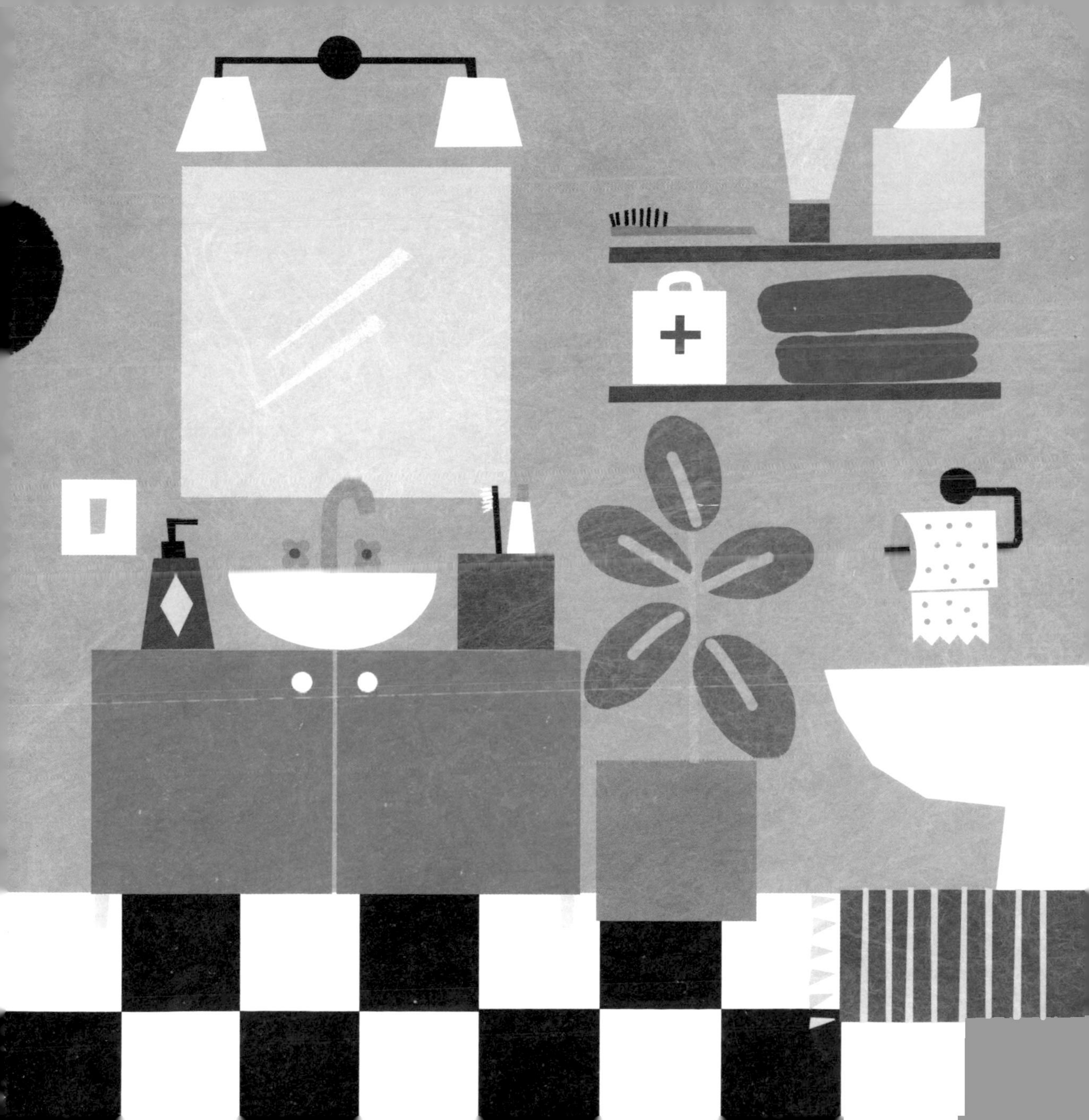

Rectangles,
rectangles!
Where are the
rectangles?

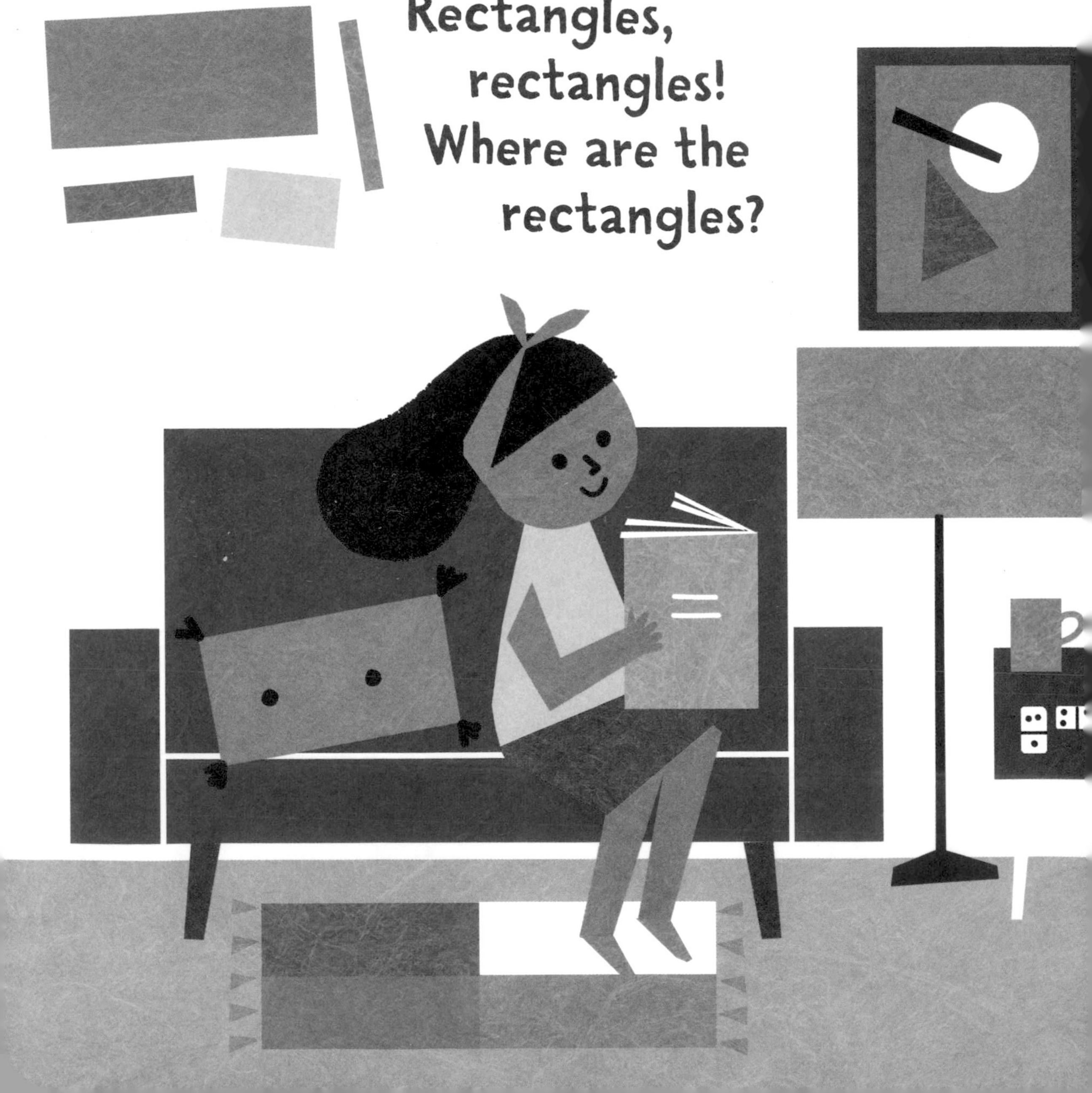

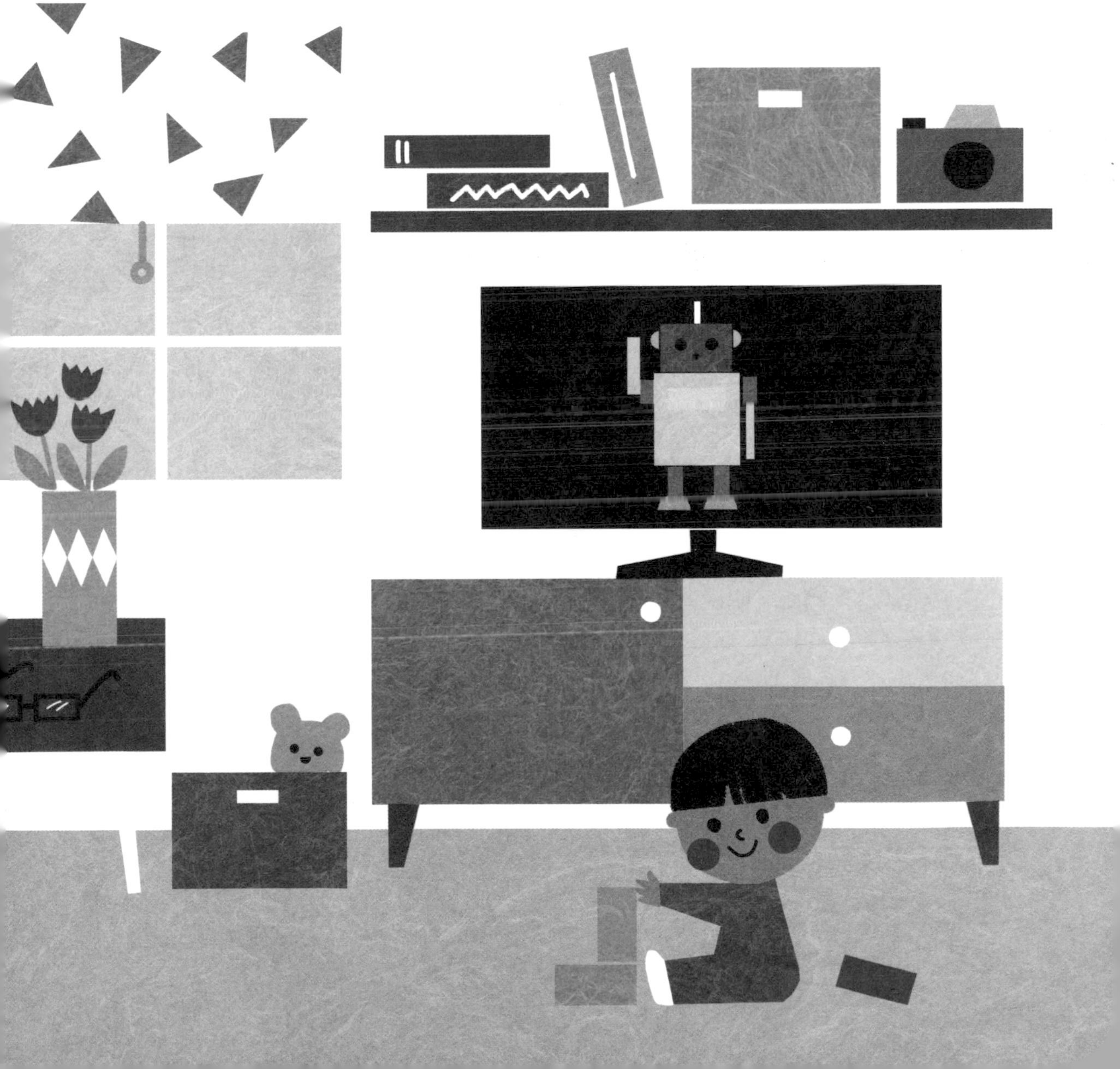

Circles, circles!
Everywhere!

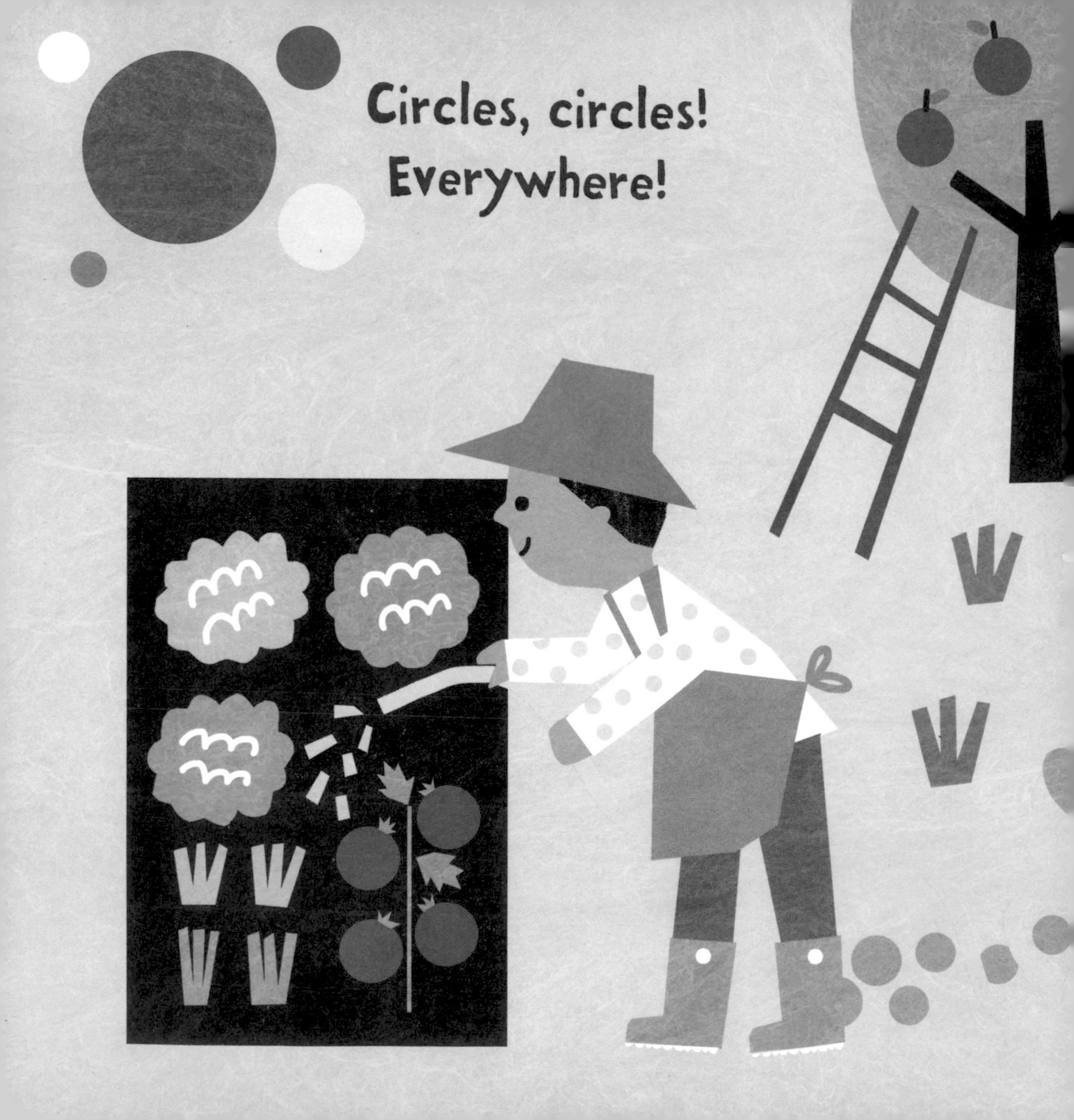

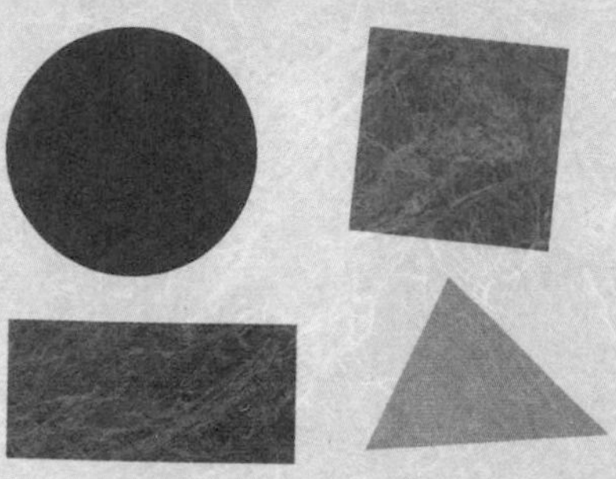

Look at all the shapes!

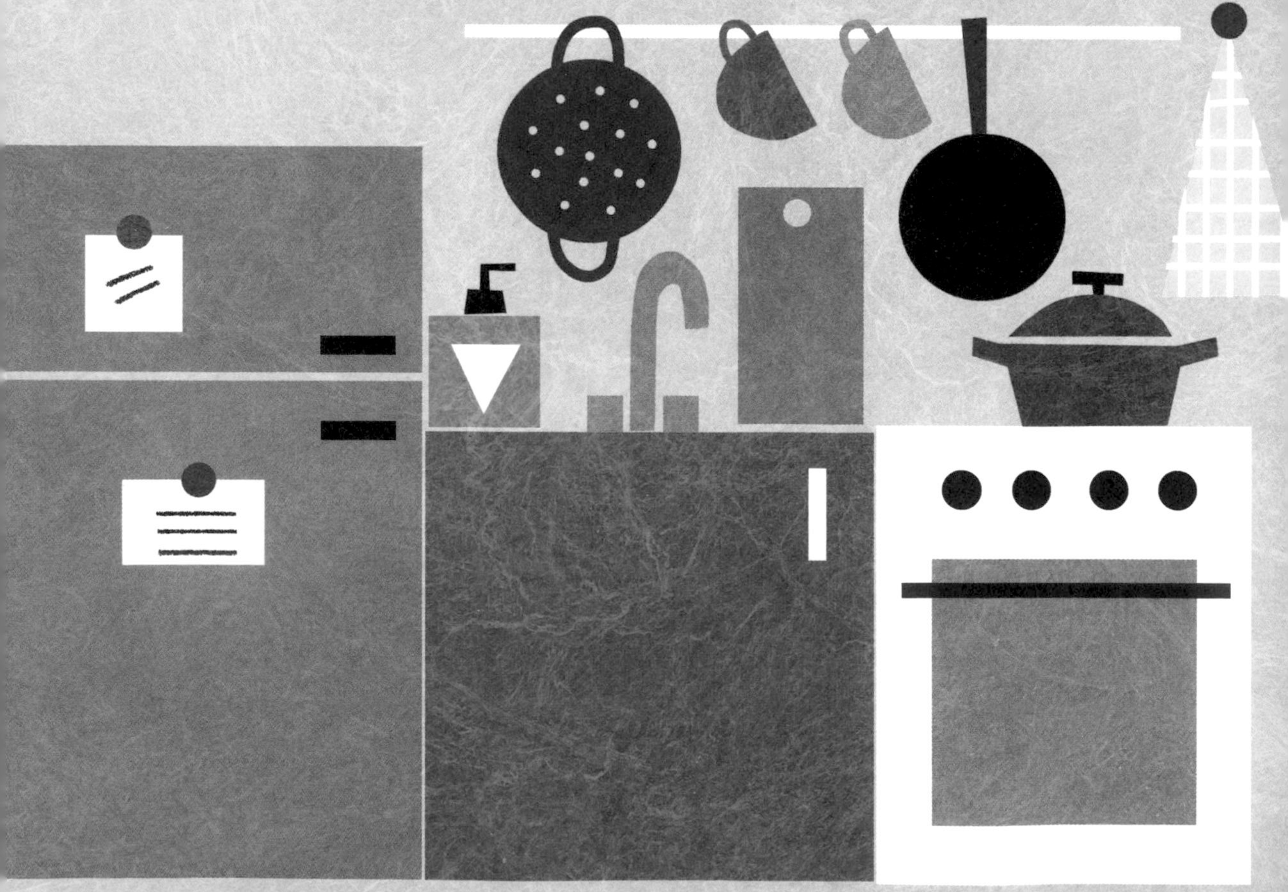